Every child is a different kind of flower,
and all together make this world a beautiful garden.

THIS BOOK BELONGS TO ....

BORN IN THE MONTH OF ....

For Alice

Copyright © 2021 by Brigette Barrager

All rights reserved. Published in the United States by Random House Children's Books,

a division of Penguin Random House LLC, New York.

Random House and the colophon are registered trademarks of Penguin Random House LLC.

Visit us on the Web! rhcbooks.com

Educators and librarians, for a variety of teaching tools,

visit us at RHTeachersLibrarians.com

Library of Congress Cataloging-in-Publication Data

Name: Barrager, Brigette, author, illustrator.

Title: Welcome flower child : the magic of your birth flower / Brigette Barrager.

Description: First edition. | New York : Random House Children's Books, [2021] | Audience: Ages 3–7. | Audience: Grades K–1. |

Summary: Illustrations and rhyming text describe the birth month flowers, including March's daffodils, June's roses,

and September's morning glories, as well as how each represents children born in that month.

Identifiers: LCCN 2019053958 (print) | LCCN 2019053959 (ebook) | ISBN 978-1-9848-3039-5 (hardcover) |

ISBN 978-1-9848-3040-1 (library binding) | ISBN 978-1-9848-3041-8 (ebook)

Subjects: CYAC: Stories in rhyme. | Birth flowers—Fiction. | Flowers—Fiction.

Classification: LCC PZ8.3.B252644 Flo 2021 (print) | LCC PZ8.3.B252644 (ebook) | DDC [E]—dc23

Interior design by Sarah Hokanson

MANUFACTURED IN CHINA   10 9 8 7 6 5 4 3 2 1   First Edition

Random House Children's Books supports the First Amendment

and celebrates the right to read.

Welcome Flower Child

The Magic of Your Birth Flower

Brigette Barrager

Random House
NEW YORK

Flowers bloom inside this book.
Turn the pages. Take a look.
A flower blooms each month anew.
Find the flower just for you.

January: Carnation

In January, the year is new
as you bring life and light with you.
The way you blossom, big and bold,
brings warmth and love to fight the cold.

February flowers, slow to unfold,
will open wide with hearts of gold.
A child with charm and dreaming eyes
brings sunshine to the grayest skies.

February: Violet

March: Daffodil

All March babes are warm and bright,
like daffodils, a spring delight.
A sunshine smile is what you bring
to make each day as fresh as spring.

April: Sweet Pea

April flowers have no fear,
born to thrive and persevere.
Sweet vines reach toward the sun.
Posies bloom and burst with fun.

Welcoming May's butterflies
are lacy bells and blushing skies.
With smiles and laughter, charm and grace,
your love feels like a warm embrace.

May: Lily of the Valley

June: Rose

The kindest babes are born in June
and shine just like the sun at noon.
Within your brambles, magic grows,
a child, lovely as a rose.

Little one born in July,
you're brilliant as a summer sky.
You bring radiant fun to every day
with a smile to send the blues away.

July: Water Lily

August: Poppy

August flowers stand up for what's just.
You're the kind of friend we all can trust.
Your tender heart is so resilient
and blooms like flowers big and brilliant.

September:
Morning Glory

Flower child born in September,
your affection is what we remember.
With warmth and magic in your heart,
your grace always sets you apart.

October's children truly care,
live to comfort, heal, and share.
A friend who knows just what to do.
Loving others is easy for you.

October: Marigold

November: Chrysanthemum

November flower, you're such fun,
giving the giggles to everyone!
As you brighten up the dusky fall,
your warmth brings smiles to us all.

December: Poinsettia

December's flowers are vibrant and strong.
They raise our spirits like a song.
Your sweetness and courage are a gift
that gives our hearts a cheerful lift.

No matter what the time of year,
you were born to be held dear.
Adventure through the garden bed.
Travel where your heart has led.
The greatest bliss I'll ever know
will be to watch you grow, grow, grow!